THE WIDE-AWAKE OWL

THE WIDE-A

WAKE OWL

LOUIS SLOBODKIN

THE MACMILLAN COMPANY

NEW YORK

FOR

NAOMI

WITH LOVE

Library of Congress catalog card number: 58–6732

© Louis Slobodkin 1958

Printed in the United States of America

Music for "Song of the Thrush"
© Michael Slobodkin 1958

THE WIDE-AWAKE OWL

Olga, the little owl, could not sleep. She was wide awake.

She tried to sleep, like all owls do, during the daytime. But she could not sleep a wink.

She tried sleeping with only one eye shut the way owls do.

Then she tried sleeping with the other eye shut.

And at last she shut both eyes as tight as she

could for a long, long time. But it was no use. The little owl could not sleep. She was wide awake.

"What shall I do?" she said to herself. "I must sleep. Everyone has to sleep."

At last Olga decided to ask the wise old owl who lived nearby what to do. She flew over to the oak tree where the wise old owl lived.

The wise old owl, with only one eye shut, was sound asleep in the bright sunlight.

"Excuse me," said Olga gently.

The wise old owl kept right on sleeping.

"Excuse me," said Olga again in a louder voice.

But the old owl kept right on sleeping.

"EXCUSE me!" screeched Olga as loud as she could.

"WHO . . .WHO . . . What's the matter?"
said the wise old owl as he woke up.

"I can't sleep," said Olga.

"Well I CAN!" said the wise old owl and went
right back to sleep again.

"Please help me," said Olga. "What shall I
do? I can't sleep a wink."

The wise old owl grumbled and half-opened
his eyes.

"Did you try sleeping with one eye shut?" he
asked.

"Yes," said Olga.

"Try it again . . . right now!" said the wise
old owl.

Again Olga shut one eye tight and tried to sleep. The wise old owl watched her a moment.

"Asleep yet?" he asked.

"No," said Olga.

"Try sleeping with the other eye shut."

Olga tried that too and after another moment the old owl asked:

"Asleep yet?"

"No," said Olga.

The old owl thought a few minutes.

"Well then," he said . . . "I don't like to advise this because owls do not usually sleep this way . . . but try sleeping with both eyes shut."

Olga shut both her eyes as tight as she could. The wise old owl watched her carefully for two long minutes. Then he shouted:

"ASLEEP YET?"

Olga's eyes popped open. She sadly shook her head.

"Well, there's no more I can do for you," said the wise old owl. And he shut one eye again and promptly went back to sleep.

Olga flew back to her own tree and perched on a branch.

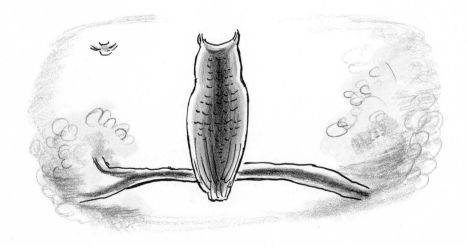

"Dear me, what shall I do? What shall I do?" said Olga.

"What do you want to do?" asked somebody.

Olga turned her head. It was a friendly chipmunk who lived higher up in her tree.

"I want to sleep," said Olga, "but I can't."

"Did you try sleeping all curled up like this?" asked the friendly chipmunk. "This is the way I sleep."

The chipmunk curled up like a tight ball of fur and fell asleep at once.

Olga curled up as best she could, closed her eyes . . .

. . . and she almost fell off the branch.

"I can't sleep that way," she said.

Just then a young possum came down the tree.

"Of course you can't sleep like that," said the possum. "I can't either. Try sleeping like this. I always do."

The possum curled his long tail firmly around the branch of the tree and hung head down. Then he smiled gently, closed his eyes and in a flash he was sound asleep.

Since Olga had no long curly tail, she took a firm grip on the branch with her claws and let herself tumble forward until she hung upside down too. She closed one eye.

Then she closed the other eye.

Then she closed both eyes tight. She tried very hard to sleep but she could not.

And again she opened her eyes.

"I can't sleep that way either," she said.

A bluejay who had been watching said, "Of course you can't. No bird can sleep like that. Here, try sleeping this way."

The bluejay tucked her head under her wing and in no time at all she was fast asleep.

Olga tried tucking her head under her wing. But her neck was so short and her head so big her wing hardly covered one eye.

"Dear me, dear me, will I ever sleep again," sighed Olga.

A robin who had been flying by stopped and sat on a twig.

"I have a good way to sleep," said the robin. "Try standing on one leg on a springy twig like this. It will rock you to sleep. Watch me."

The robin stood on one leg and the twig rocked up and down once . . . twice and be-

fore anyone could count to three fast . . . the robin was asleep.

Olga looked along the branch where she stood until she saw another little twig. She hopped onto the twig and stood on one leg. Then she bounced to make the twig rock. She bounced once . . . then twice, and on the third bounce, because Olga was too heavy for the twig . . .

. . . the twig broke!

And Olga went crashing down through the branches of the tree! And she could not get her wings spread in time to keep from bumping on the ground when she landed.

A little thrush flew down from somewhere.

"What happened?" he cried. "Find something good to eat?"

"I wasn't looking for something to eat," said Olga. "I was trying to fall asleep."

"That's a funny way to fall asleep," said the thrush — "falling down through a tree that way."

By this time the little animals and birds who had been showing Olga how to go to sleep were awakened by the sound of her fall and they all rushed down from the tree.

"Are you hurt?" they cried.

Olga shook her head. "No, I'm not . . . And I still haven't been able to go to sleep."

Then Olga quickly explained to the thrush all the ways she had tried to go to sleep. . . . Like the chipmunk all curled up and like the possum hanging head down and like the blue-jay with her head tucked under her wing and like the robin standing one-legged on a swinging twig . . .

"Oh," said the thrush, "so you want to GO to sleep! I know the best way to GO to sleep . . . Come on back up into the tree."

So Olga and the other birds and animals went back up into the tree with the thrush.

The sun was just beginning to set and the woods were beginning to darken.

"Now," said the thrush, when they were all settled, "this is the best time of the day to go to sleep. And this is the best way to go to sleep . . . Go to sleep singing. Sing a low, sweet song and you will go to sleep in a jiffy."

Then the thrush began to sing a low, sweet song and all the others joined in:

MUSIC BY MICHAEL SLOBODKIN

Sweet and low To sleep we

go, The day is done, The sett...ing

sun Brings on the night, Shut both eyes

tight, The woods are still, We'll sleep un-

til, The morn-ing bright, Brings back the

light, The moon doth wane We'll wake A...

And Olga and the other birds and animals never learned the end of the thrush's song because she and all the others fell fast asleep.

From then on, whenever Olga the little owl
was wide awake and found it hard to go to sleep,
she half-closed her eyes and sang softly to herself the thrush's song . . . or as much of the
song as she knew.

And she always fell asleep before she came to the end of the song so she never really had to know how it ended.

THE END